WHERE'S WALDO?
THE WONDER BOOK

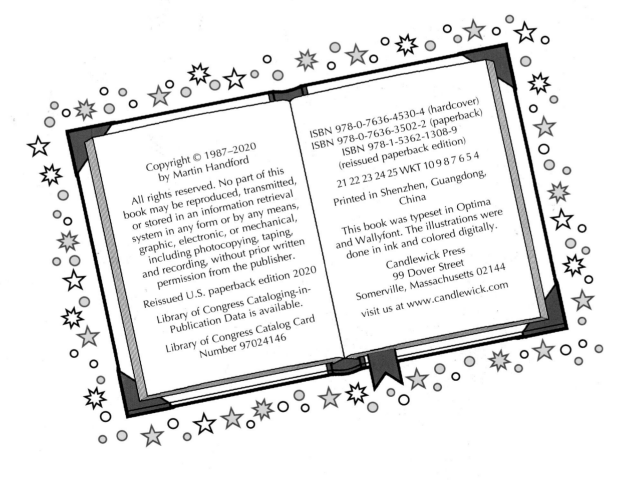

Reissued U.S. paperback edition 2020

Library of Congress Cataloging-in-
Publication Data is available.

Library of Congress Catalog Card
Number 97024146

ISBN 978-0-7636-4530-4 (hardcover)
ISBN 978-0-7636-3502-2 (paperback)
ISBN 978-1-5362-1308-9
(reissued paperback edition)

21 22 23 24 25 WKT 10 9 8 7 6 5 4

Printed in Shenzhen, Guangdong,
China

This book was typeset in Optima
and Wallyfont. The illustrations were
done in ink and colored digitally.

Candlewick Press
99 Dover Street
Somerville, Massachusetts 02144

visit us at www.candlewick.com

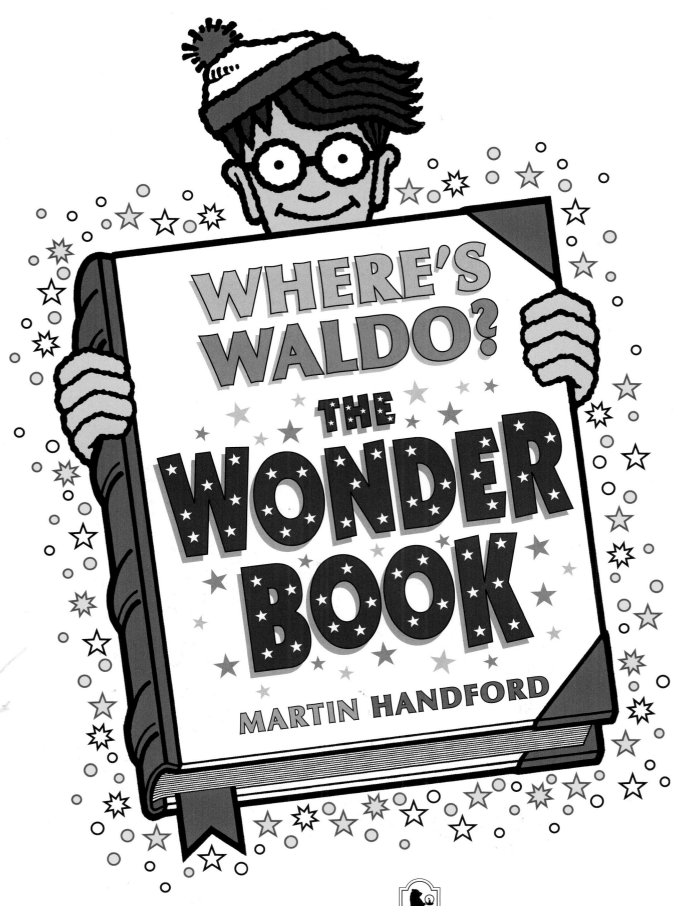

WHERE'S WALDO?
THE WONDER BOOK

MARTIN HANDFORD

Candlewick Press

Once Upon a Page...

HEY, WALDO FANS! LOOK AT ALL THESE BRILLIANT BOOKS! LOOK AT ALL THE CHARACTERS WHO HAVE STEPPED OUT FROM THEIR PAGES! WOW! WHAT A MAGIC SCENE! THESE BOOKS HAVE REALLY COME ALIVE! FANTASTIC—THAT BOOK OVER THERE IS ABOUT MY TRAVELS! AND WOOF, WENDA, WIZARD WHITEBEARD, AND ODLAW ALL HAVE SPECIAL BOOKS OF THEIR OWN. NOW YOU CAN JOIN US TOO, IF YOU CAN FIND US, AND WE'LL TRAVEL TOGETHER THROUGH ALL THE OTHER WONDERFUL SCENES IN THIS WONDER BOOK. ONE SCENE IS MY SPECIAL FAVORITE—YOU'LL NEVER GUESS WHAT MAKES IT SO GREAT. THE BOOKMARK MARKS IT, SO WHEN WE GET THERE, YOU WILL KNOW. NOW GET SEARCHING, WALDO-FOLLOWERS, AND OFF WE GO! AND BE PREPARED FOR LOTS OF SURPRISES ALONG THE WAY!

Waldo

THE SEARCH IS ON! FIND THESE FIVE INTREPID TRAVELERS IN EVERY SCENE IN THE WONDER BOOK!

- FIND WALDO . . . WHO LEADS THE WAY!
- FIND WOOF . . . WHO WAGS HIS TAIL! (WHICH IS USUALLY ALL YOU CAN SEE!)
- FIND WENDA . . . WHO TAKES THE PICTURES!
- FIND WIZARD WHITEBEARD . . . WHO CASTS THE SPELLS!
- FIND ODLAW . . . WHOSE GOOD DEEDS ARE FEW INDEED!

THE SEARCH CONTINUES! NEXT FIND THESE IMPORTANT THINGS THE TRAVELERS HAVE LOST!

- FIND WALDO'S LOST KEY!
- FIND WOOF'S LOST BONE!
- FIND WENDA'S LOST CAMERA!
- FIND WIZARD WHITEBEARD'S MAGIC SCROLL!
- FIND ODLAW'S LOST BINOCULARS!

THE GREAT BOOK OF ODLAW'S GOOD DEEDS

CLASSIC STORIES FROM LITERATURE

THE BOOK OF NURSERY RHYMES

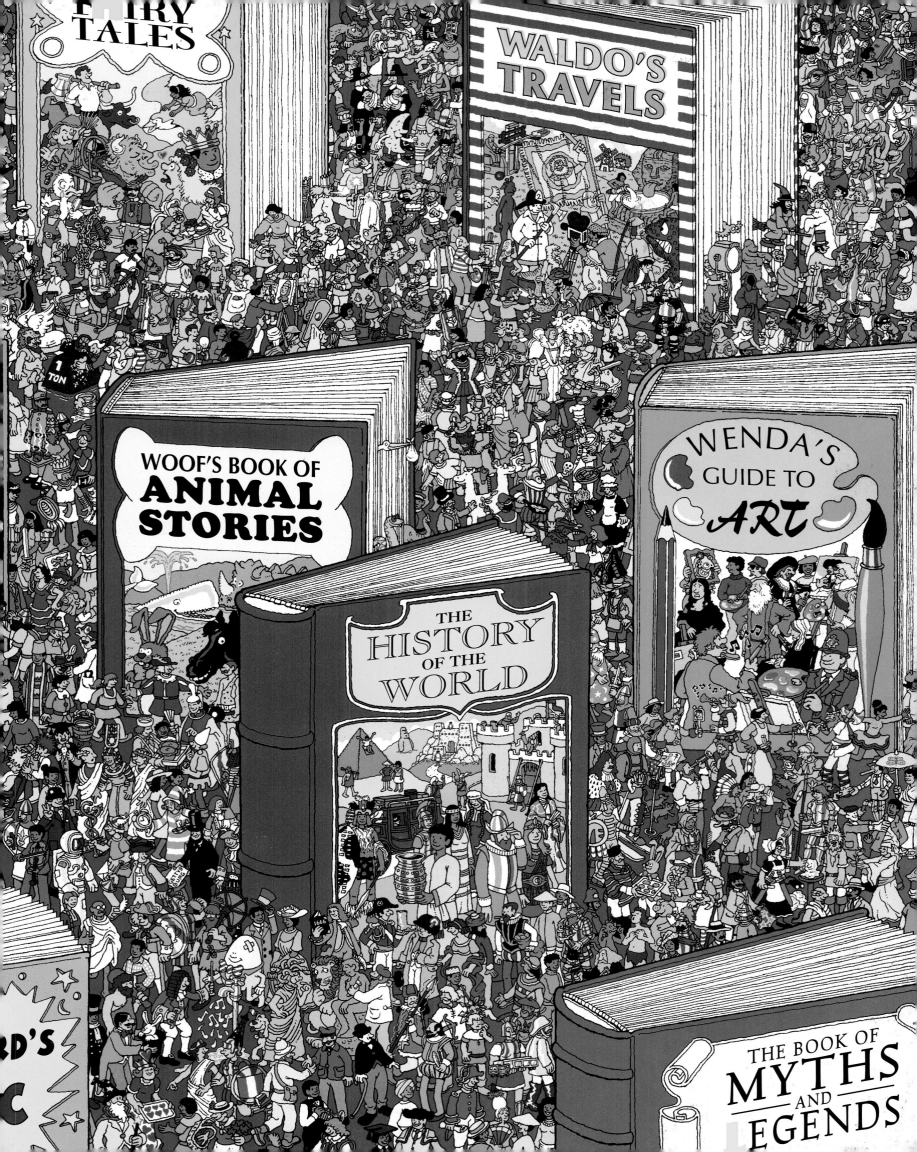

THE GAME OF GAMES

FOUR HUGE TEAMS ARE PLAYING THIS GREAT GAME OF GAMES. THE REFEREES ARE TRYING TO SEE THAT NO ONE BREAKS THE RULES. BETWEEN THE STARTING LINE AT THE TOP AND THE FINISH LINE AT THE BOTTOM, THERE ARE LOTS OF PUZZLES, BOOBY TRAPS, AND TESTS. THE GREEN TEAM'S NEARLY WON, AND THE ORANGE TEAM'S HARDLY STARTED! CAN YOU SPOT THE ONLY ORANGE TEAM PLAYER WHO HAS FINISHED? AND THE ONLY GREEN TEAM PLAYER WHO HAS NOT YET BEGUN?

THE CAKE FACTORY

OOZING SUGAR ICING AND THE SHINY RED CHERRIES ON THE ROOF UP THERE! THAT ROOM IS WHERE THE FACTORY CONTROLLERS WORK, BUT HAVE THEY LOST CONTROL?

MMMM! FEAST YOUR EYES, WALDO-WATCHERS! SNIFF THE DELICIOUS SMELLS OF BAKING CAKES! DROOL AT THE TASTY TOPPINGS! CAN YOU SEE A CAKE LIKE A TEAPOT, A CAKE LIKE A HOUSE, A CAKE SO TALL A WORKER ON THE FLOOR ABOVE IS LICKING IT? CAKES, CAKES, EVERYWHERE! HOW SCRUMPTIOUS! HOW YUM-YUM-YUMPTIOUS! LOOK AT THE

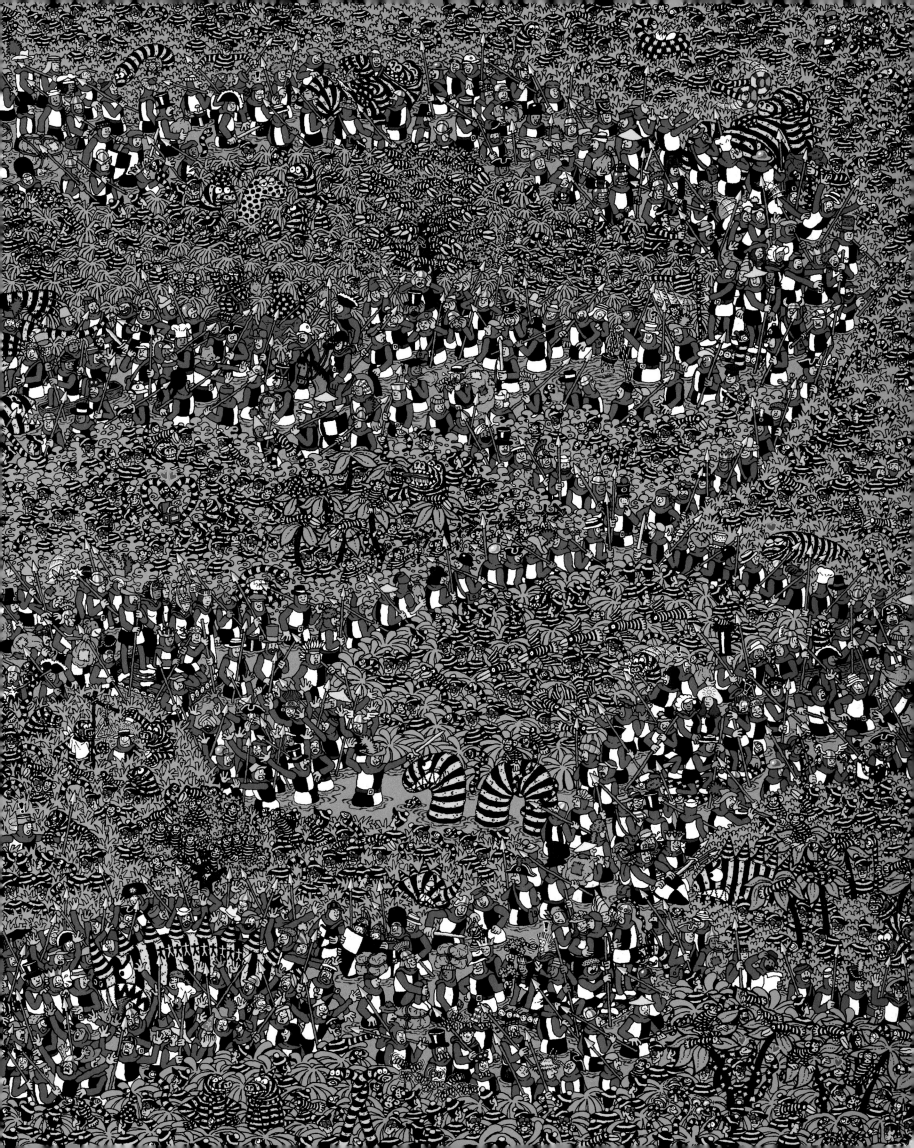

THE FANTASTIC FLOWER GARDEN

WOW! WHAT A BRIGHT AND DAZZLING GARDEN SPECTACLE! ALL THE FLOWERS ARE IN FULL BLOOM, AND HUNDREDS OF BUSY GARDENERS ARE WATERING AND TENDING THEM. THE PETAL COSTUMES THEY ARE WEARING MAKE THEM LOOK LIKE FLOWERS THEMSELVES! VEGETABLES ARE GROWING IN THE GARDEN TOO. HOW MANY DIFFERENT KINDS

CAN YOU SEE? SNIFF THE AIR, WALDO-FOLLOWERS! SMELL THE FANTASTIC SCENTS! WHAT A TREAT FOR YOUR NOSES AS WELL AS YOUR EYES!

THE CORRIDORS OF TIME

TICK-TOCK, TICK-TOCK! THE HANDS OF ALL THE CLOCKS EXCEPT ONE SAY A QUARTER TO TWELVE. WHAT A DING-DONG THERE WILL BE WHEN THEY STRIKE! CAN YOU FIND THE ONLY CLOCK THAT TELLS A DIFFERENT TIME? IN THIS SCENE ARE THIRTY-NINE DOORS. ABOVE EACH DOOR APPEARS THE SHAPE OF THE KEY THAT WILL UNLOCK IT. CAN YOU FIND THE KEYS IN THE CROWD, BRAINY ONES, AND MATCH THEM TO THE SHAPES? OH, NO! ONE DOOR HAS NO SHAPE ABOVE IT! EVEN SO, YOU MUST FIND ITS KEY!

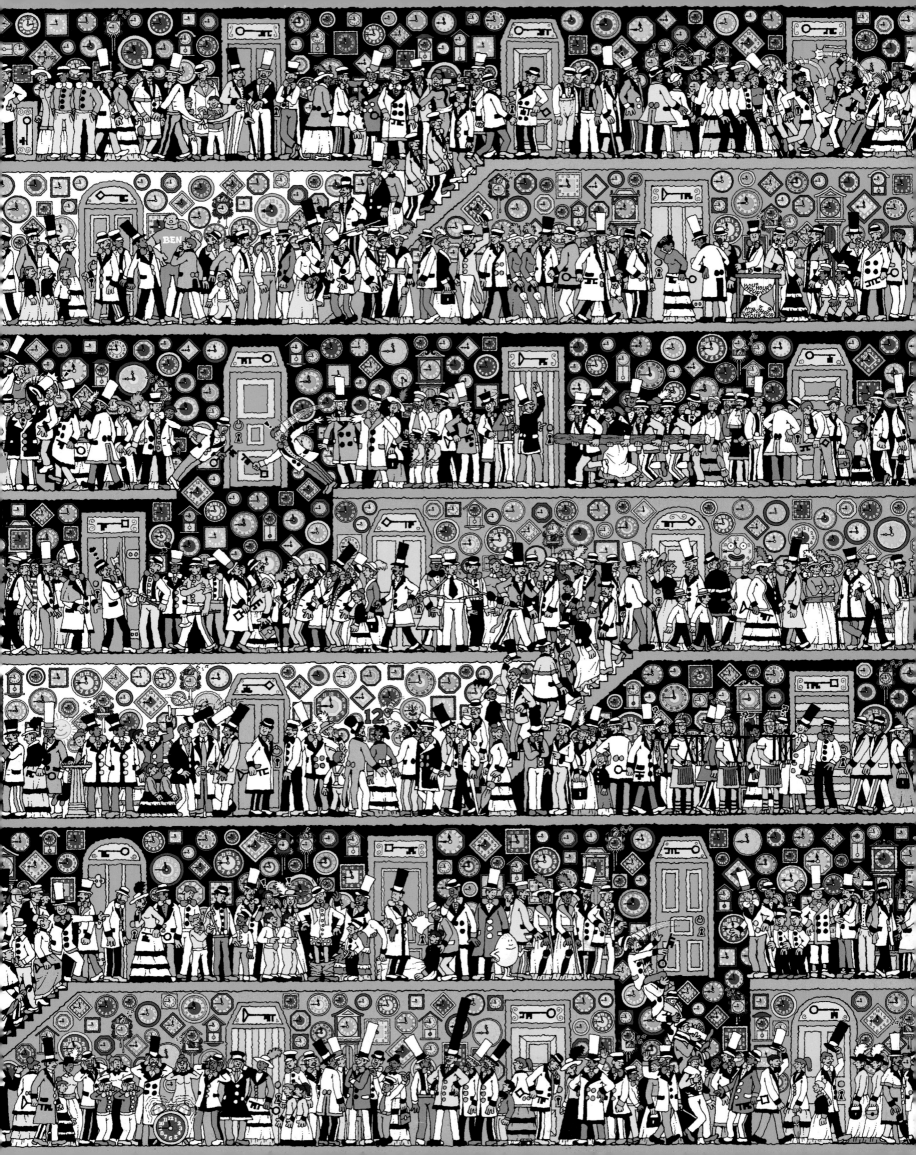

THE LAND OF WOOFS

HEY! LOOK AT ALL THESE DOGS THAT ARE DRESSED LIKE WOOF! BOW WOW WOW! IN THIS LAND, A DOG'S LIFE IS THE HIGHLIFE! THERE'S A LUXURY WOOF HOTEL WITH A BONE-SHAPED SWIMMING POOL, AND AT THE WOOF RACETRACK, LOTS OF WOOFS ARE CHASING ATTENDANTS DRESSED AS CATS, SAUSAGES, AND POSTMEN! THE BOOKMARK IS ON THIS PAGE, WALDO-FOLLOWERS. SO NOW YOU KNOW, THIS IS MY FAVORITE SCENE! THIS IS THE ONLY SCENE IN THE BOOK WHERE YOU CAN SEE MORE OF THE REAL WOOF THAN JUST HIS TAIL! BUT CAN YOU FIND HIM? HE'S THE ONLY ONE WITH FIVE RED STRIPES ON HIS TAIL! HERE'S ANOTHER CHALLENGE! ELEVEN TRAVELERS HAVE FOLLOWED ME HERE—ONE FROM EVERY SCENE. CAN YOU SEE THEM? AND CAN YOU FIND WHERE EACH ONE JOINED ME ON MY ADVENTURES, AND SPOT ALL THEIR APPEARANCES AFTERWARD? KEEP ON SEARCHING, WALDO FANS! HAVE A WONDERFUL, WONDERFUL TIME!

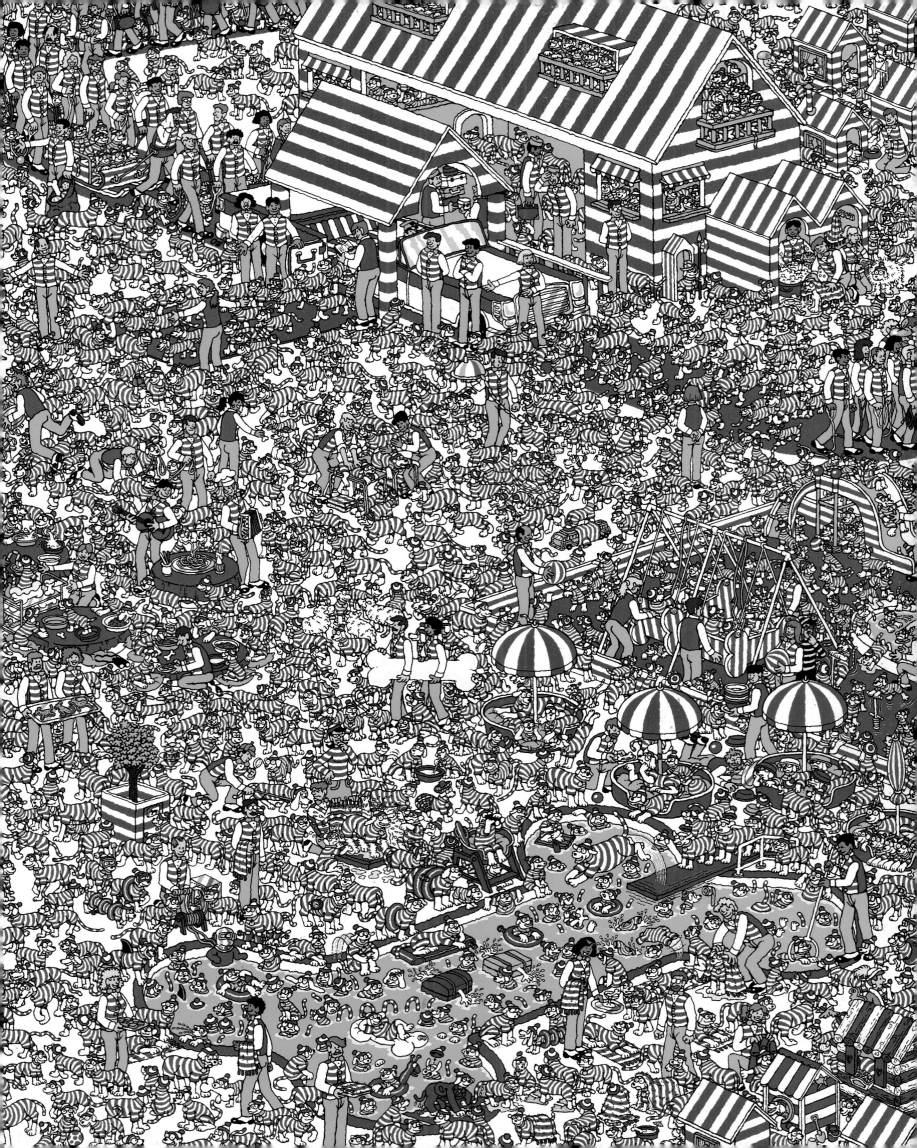

THE GREAT
WHERE'S WALDO?
THE WONDER BOOK
CHECKLIST

More and more wonderful things for Waldo fans to check out!

ONCE UPON A PAGE . . .

- Helen of Troy and Paris
- Rudyard Kipling and the jungle book
- Sir Francis and his drake
- Wild Bill hiccup
- A shopping centaur
- Handel's water music
- George washing ton
- Samuel peeps at his diary
- Guy forks
- Tchaikovsky and the nut cracker sweet
- A Roundhead with a round head
- Pythagoras and the square of the hippopotamus
- William shakes spear
- Madame two swords
- Garibaldi and his biscuits
- Florence and her nightingale
- The pilgrim fathers
- Captain cook
- Hamlet making an omelet
- Jason and the juggernauts
- Whistling Whistler painting his mother
- The Queen of Hearts
- Lincoln and the Gettysburg address
- Stephenson's rocket
- Two knights fighting the war of the roses
- The Duke of Wellington's wellington

THE MIGHTY FRUIT FIGHT

- A box of dates next to a box of dates
- A pair of date palms
- "An apple a day keeps the doctor away!"
- Six crab apples
- Four naval oranges
- Blueberries wearing blue berets
- A kiwi fruit
- A banana doing a split
- A pine apple
- Three fruit fools
- A bowl of fruit and a can of fruit
- Cranberry saws
- An orange upsetting the apple cart
- A banana tree
- Cooking apples
- Elder berry wine
- Seven wild cherries
- Goose berries
- A pound of apples
- A partridge in a pear tree
- A fruit cock tail
- Two peach halves
- "The Big Apple"
- One sour apple without a beard
- Paw paw fruit
- Another apple cart being upset

CLOWN TOWN

- A clown reading a newspaper
- A starry umbrella
- A clown with a blue teapot
- Two hoses leaking
- A clown with two hoops on each arm
- A clown looking through a telescope
- Two clowns holding big hammers
- A clown with a bag of party favors
- Two clowns holding flowerpots
- A clown swinging a pillow
- A clown combing the roof of a Clown Town house
- A clown bursting a balloon
- Six flowers squirting the same clown
- A clown wearing a jack-in-the-box hat
- Three cars
- Three watering cans
- A clown with a fishing rod
- One hat joining two clowns
- Clowns wearing tea shirts
- A clown having his foot tickled
- Three clowns with buckets of water
- A clown with a yo-yo
- A clown stepping into a custard pie
- Seventeen clouds
- A clown about to catapult a custard pie
- One clown with a green nose

THE ODLAW SWAMP

- Two soldiers disguised as Odlaws
- A soldier wearing a bowler hat
- A soldier wearing a stovepipe hat
- A soldier wearing a riding helmet
- A soldier wearing a straw hat
- Three soldiers wearing peaked caps
- A lady wearing an Easter bonnet
- Two soldiers wearing football helmets
- Two soldiers wearing baseball caps
- A big shield next to a little shield
- A lady wearing a sun hat
- A soldier with two big feathers in his hat
- Some rattle snakes
- Five romantic snakes
- Seven wooden rafts
- Three small wooden boats
- Four birds' nests
- One Odlaw in disguise
- A swamp creature without stripes
- A monster cleaning its teeth
- A monster asleep, but not for long
- A soldier floating on a package
- A very big monster with a very small head
- One charmed snake
- Five charmed spears
- A snake reading

THE FANTASTIC FLOWER GARDEN

- The yellow rose of Texas
- Flowerpots and flower beds
- Butter flies
- Gardeners sewing seeds and planting bulbs
- A garden nursery
- A bird bath and a bird table
- House plants, wall flowers, and blue bells
- Dandy lions, tiger lilies, and fox gloves
- Cabbage patches, letters leaves, and a collie flower
- A hedgehog next to a hedge hog
- A flower border and a flower show
- A bull frog
- Earth worms
- A wheelbarrow full of wheels
- A cricket match
- Parsley, sage, Rosemary, and time
- A queen bee near a honey comb
- A landscape gardener
- A sun dial next to a sundial
- Gardeners dancing to the beetles
- A green house and a tree house
- A spring onion and a leek with a leak
- Door mice
- An apple tree
- Weeping willows and climbing roses
- Rock pool

THE CORRIDORS OF TIME

- The clock striking twelve
- Clock faces
- Wall clocks
- An egg timer
- A clock tower
- A very loud alarm clock
- A traveling clock
- A runner racing against time
- Roman numerals
- Time flies
- An hour glass
- Big Ben
- Old Father Time
- Grandfather clocks
- A walking stick
- Thirty-six pairs of almost identical twins
- One pair of identical twins
- A man's suspenders being pulled in opposite directions
- A swinging pendulum
- Coattails tied in a knot
- A door and thirteen clocks on their sides
- A very tall top hat
- A sundial
- A pair of hooked umbrellas
- A clock cuckoo
- A pair of tangled walking sticks

THE GAME OF GAMES

Some stair cases
Maize inside a maze
A cross word
A flight of stairs
A map reading
A player rolling the dice
A tightrope walking
A player with a map and a pair of compasses
A player throwing a six
One player not wearing gloves
One lost glove
The other lost glove
A missing puzzle piece
A bad mathematician
Eight shovels
Twenty-nine hoops
Two cans of paint
An upside-down question mark on a player's tunic
A blue player holding a green block
A player with a magnet
Five referees with their arms folded
Five crying players with handkerchiefs
Two players reading newspapers
A smoke signal
Three ticklish players
Eight messages in bottles

TOYS! TOYS! TOYS!

Two spinning tops and a top spinning
Jack in a box
A jack in a box
A toy soldier being decorated
A toy soldier in full dress uniform
A toy drill sergeant
A fish tank
Four baby's bottles
Two anchors
A toy figure on skis
A chalkboard
A toy figure pushing a wheelbarrow
A crow's-nest
An apple tree bookend
A goal
Five big red books
A bear on a rocking horse
A toy bandsman holding cymbals
A toy performer balancing two chairs in the air
Five wooden ladders
A giraffe with a red-and-white striped scarf
A pirate carrying a barrel
Toy figures climbing up a long scarf
A teddy bear wearing a green scarf
Two giraffes in the ark
A robot holding a red tray

BRIGHT LIGHTS AND NIGHT FRIGHTS

Street lights
Lime light
A rowboat
An octo-puss
Moon light
Light entertainers
A very light house
Day light
A fishing boat
A standard lamp
Christmas tree lights
A light weight boxer
Star light
A light at the end of the tunnel
Stage lights
A motorboat
A sailor walking the plank
A diving board
Candle light
A bedside light
The deep blue C
A Chinese lantern
A search light
A sleeping monster
A mirror
Four sailors looking through telescopes

THE BATTLE OF THE BANDS

A rubber band
A piano forty
A pipe band
Bandsmen "playing" their instruments
A fan fair
Bandsmen with saxophones and sacks of phones
A steel band
A swing band
Sheet music
Racing bandsmen "beating" their drums
A rock band
Kettle drums
A mouth organ
A baby sitar
A 1-man band
A French horn
A barrel organ
Some violin bows
A rock and roll band
Bandsmen playing cornets
A drummer with drumsticks
A big elephant trunk
Bandsmen making a drum kit
The orchestra pit
A bag piper
Some cheetah bandsmen cheating

THE CAKE FACTORY

A loading bay
Conveyor belts
Two Danish pastries
A gingerbread man
Two workers blowing cream horns
Maple syrup
Hot cross buns
A Viennese whirl
A Swiss roll
A pan cake
A chocolate moose
A custard-pie fight
Apple pie
A black forest cake
A fish cake
Rock cakes
Two kinds of dough nuts
A doe nut
Baked Alaska pudding
A fairy cake
Mississippi mud pie
Upside-down cake
Carrot cake
A cup cake
Sponge cakes
A cake carrying a worker

THE LAND OF WOOFS

Dog biscuits
A mountain dog
A hot dog getting cool
A gray hound bus
Dog baskets
A pair of swimming trunks
A sheep dog
A watch dog
A bull dog
A great Dane
A guard dog
A dog in a wet suit
Some swimming costumes
A dog with a red collar
A dog wearing a yellow collar with a blue tag
A dog with a blue pom-pom on his hat
A top dog
A sausage dog with sausages
A dog wearing a blue collar with a green tag
A cat dressed like a Woof dog
The puppies' pool
A Woof doing a paw stand
A Scottie dog
Two dogs getting a massage
A sniffer dog
Twenty-two red-and-white striped towels

★ ★ ★ ★ SEEING STARS! ★ ★ ★ ★

Now it's the end, it's time to go back to the beginning!
Remember the first two pages of the book with all
the pretty colored stars on them? Can you spot ten
differences between the pictures in the shapes on the
left and the pictures in the shapes on the right? And
can you find one star shape and one circle shape that
both appear four times?

CLOWNING ABOUT!

Ha, ha! What a joker! The clown who follows
Waldo and his friends to the end of the book
changes the color of his hat band in one scene!
Can you find which scene it is? What color
does his hat band change to?

One last thing…